MASTER YOUR DESTINY

THE PIRATE'S
CURSE

With special thanks to Elizabeth Galloway

To Leo Heppell

www.beastquest.co.uk

ORCHARD BOOKS
338 Euston Road, London NW1 3BH
Orchard Books Australia
Level 17/207 Kent St, Sydney, NSW 2000

A Paperback Original
First published in Great Britain in 2012

Beast Quest is a registered trademark of Beast Quest Limited
Series created by Beast Quest Limited, London

Text © Beast Quest Limited 2012
Cover and inside illustrations by Steve Sims © Beast Quest Limited 2012

A CIP catalogue record for this book is available from
the British Library.

ISBN 978 1 40831 840 9

5 7 9 10 8 6

Printed and bound by CPI Group (UK) Ltd, Croydon, CR0 4YY

The paper and board used in this paperback are natural recyclable
products made from wood grown in sustainable forests. The
manufacturing processes conform to the environmental regulations of
the country of origin.

Orchard Books is a division of Hachette Children's Books,
an Hachette UK company

www.hachette.co.uk

THE PIRATE'S CURSE

BY ADAM BLADE

ORCHARD

Greetings, landlubber!

I'm Sanpao the Pirate King – and I'm sailing to Avantia.

I'm sure you would rather forget the time my crew terrorized the land! It was fun until Tom drove me and my six Beasts away.

But I'm back and I've used my magic to create two new Beasts. Polkai the Shark-Man and Dredda the Tunnelling Menace.

But what's this? Word has arrived of a new Quester determined to stop me: YOU! Prepare yourself for deadly duels, plundering pirates and battling Beasts. Our course is set. Full speed to Avantia!

Sanpao the Pirate King

1

"Whoa, Lightning!" you say to your white horse. She whinnies and draws to a halt, her hooves skidding on the stony ground of Avantia's Central Plains. Tom pulls up beside you on Storm, his faithful stallion. Elenna is sat behind him.

"What is it?" Tom asks.

"Over there." You point towards the jagged purple outline of the Northern Mountains. Hanging over them is a dark shape, suspended in the sky.

"Maybe it's just a rain cloud," Elenna suggests.

"But I've never seen a cloud like that," you reply. "Let's take a closer look."

You turn Lightning towards the mountains. Silver, Elenna's pet wolf, is several paces away. She whistles to him, and with a howl he follows the horses.

Tom and Elenna are helping you become a knight of Avantia. As part of your training, you must prove that you can defend the kingdom from danger. *Maybe*

I'm about to get my chance, you think.

After a while, the ground slopes steeply upward and you lead the way into the mountain peaks. Above you, the strange object sways in the air like a distant ship at sea.

"I remember seeing a village around here on one of my Quests," says Tom. "I think that thing is floating right above it."

The horses' hooves clatter as you weave through rocks and boulders. But soon the sound is masked by shouts and screams of fear.

You turn to Tom and Elenna. "The village must be under attack. Hurry!"

Lightning gallops through a narrow passageway, and you emerge into a ruined village square. A gang of men upturn market stalls and smash windows, while the villagers cower in fear.

The men's heads are partly shaved, with long, greasy pigtails hanging down their backs. They wear heavy boots and sleeveless jerkins, and on each of their arms is a skull tattoo.

"I've seen these thugs before," says
Tom grimly. "They're pirates!"

One of them emerges from a house
with a sack full of goblets and ornaments.
Another pirate snatches the pendant from
a woman's neck.

"Enough!" you yell, and jump down from
Lightning. You draw your sword, but before
you can charge the pirates, the sky darkens.
The vast floating object in the sky is sinking
down to earth.

"It's a pirate ship," you gasp.

As it glides lower and lower, you realise
that you must make the first choice of your
Quest.

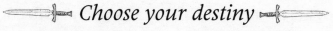 *Choose your destiny*

To wait for the ship to land, turn to **23**.

To help the villagers, turn to **34**.

2

"Whoa!" you cry as you topple into a stream of rapids. *It's like Aduro always says*, you think. *Out of the cauldron, into the fire...*

The water sweeps you and Elenna along. Silver and Lightning sprint along the edge of the stream, following after you.

The rapids spit you out into a green pool. It's edged by pillars of rock that are covered in gems. They shine like coloured stars – yellow, purple and blue – and remind you of the Fire Stone.

"Maybe they've got magical powers too," says Elenna, bobbing beside you.

You swim over to look at a pillar studded with yellow crystals. But something suddenly tugs at your leg and you can't move.

I must be caught in some weeds! you think, and duck under the surface to free yourself.

To your horror, you see that a huge jellyfish is gripping your leg. It hangs like a transparent mushroom, its tentacles

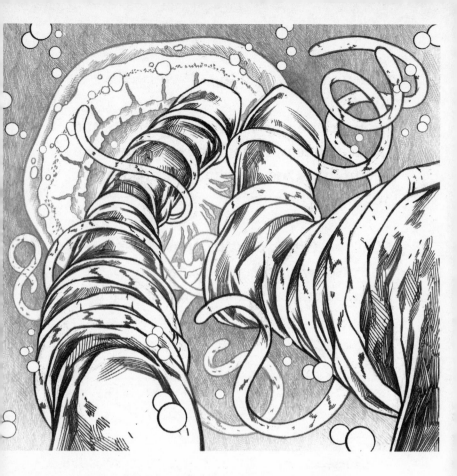

wrapped around your boot. There are
hundreds of other jellyfish in the water,
stretching out their tentacles towards you.

Your heart thumping, you pull your
sword from its scabbard and plunge it into
the jellyfish's body. With a hissing sound, it
shrivels up and you pull your leg free. You
burst back to the surface.

"Elenna, we've got to go!" you yell. "Jellyfish!"

Your friend starts to swim for shore. But after a couple of strokes she stops and gasps with fright. "One of them's got my arm. I'm trapped!"

Choose your destiny

To stay and free Elenna, turn to **43**

To get to the shore and save yourself, turn to **26**

3

From out of the shuddering ground erupts one of the most terrifying Beasts you've ever seen. Her body is like a gigantic snake, thicker than a tree trunk and rippling with muscle. Diamond claws hang from her four gigantic feet. Her head tapers to a deadly point made of bone.

This is Sanpao's servant, Dredda the Tunnelling Menace, says a familiar voice. Aduro! The Good Wizard's words float around you. *Her most deadly weapon is her skull...*

As Aduro's warning fades, Dredda rears up in front of you. She roars, revealing huge molar teeth, then slams her head down. You scramble out of the way and her skull pierces the ground where you were standing, as easily as a sword through water.

Tom's face turns red as he lifts up a rock. "I'm going to ram this in her jaws," he pants.

Dredda lunges her tapered skull towards him, roaring, and Tom lodges the rock into her open mouth. But the Beast crunches through it, her teeth grinding the rock to powder.

"We may need help defeating her," Tom says. "Shall I use my shield to summon Tagus the Horse-Man?"

⊰⊱ Choose your destiny ⊰⊱

To fight Dredda without help, turn to **9**

To call for Tagus, turn to **16**

4

Silver bounds along the rocky mountainside. Lightning stays close behind him, carrying you and Elenna. Every few moments, the wolf pauses to sniff the trail.

You round a bend and gasp.

Stretched before you is a dazzling mountain lake, with a forest at one end and a steep cliff at the other. Beside the lake, locked in battle, are two Beasts.

One is huge, with matted hair all over his body. His single eye is narrowed in anger as he swings a clawed fist at his opponent.

"That's Arcta the Mountain Giant – one of the Good Beasts," says Elenna. "But who's he fighting?"

The other Beast is part-skeleton, part-shark. From the back of his skull grows a fin and he carries a serrated cutlass.

"He must be one of Sanpao's Beasts,"
you reply. "We've got to help Arcta!"
But what is the best way to attack?

⟨══⊰⊱── *Choose your destiny* ──⊰⊱══⟩
To attack from the forest, turn to **19**
To attack from the cliff, turn to **49**

5

By the side of the lake is a clump of
seaweed draped over something wooden.
You sweep the green tendrils aside to reveal
a small rowing boat. A pair of oars lie in the
bottom, along with two fishing spears.

"Perfect for catching a Shark-Man!"
you say.

Leaving the horses and Silver on the
shore, you and Tom drag the boat into the
lake. Elenna clambers onboard and takes
the oars. "My Uncle Leo taught me how
to row," she says. You and Tom climb in,
and with strong strokes she directs the boat
towards Polkai.

The Shark-Man dives beneath the
surface. Holding one of the spears, you
peer into the water. "I can't see him,"
you mutter.

"Look out!" yells Tom. Polkai's cutlass
thrusts through the bottom of the boat.
Water pours through the hole.

"We're going to sink!" Elenna cries.

"We don't have long…"

A dark shape emerges from under the boat. The Beast! You plunge your spear into it.

Polkai surfaces, his face contorted with pain. Your strike has torn his fin.

He swims towards the shore, and Elenna follows. The Beast drags himself onto the sand and lies gasping for breath.

"Please," Polkai begs. "Let me live!"

━━┥ Choose your destiny ┝━

To let Polkai live, turn to **21**

To defeat Polkai, turn to **52**

6

You step through the waterfall into a dark tunnel. The flickering orbs of light make it difficult to see, and you rest your hand on your sword hilt.

A growl sounds in the darkness.

"A Beast!" Tom hisses.

But a familiar voice calls out. "It's me, Elenna! And Silver, too!"

You grin with relief, and together go through the rest of the tunnel. You emerge beside a vast lake. Bright red crabs scuttle through weeds that sprout between the rocks.

Praaaannnggg! A cutlass slams into the ground, just missing your foot. You gasp when you see that it's been hurled by a terrifying Beast, crouched by the edge of the lake. His skeleton body has patches of grey skin and on the back of his skull-like head is a fin. "I am Polkai the Shark Man," he snarls, revealing rows of deadly teeth. "And I challenge you to fight me!"

Polkai dives into the lake. You're determined to defeat the Beast – but should you fight him in the water? Your eye catches the abandoned shell of one of the red crabs. *Perhaps I could pretend it's the Fire Stone, and lure Polkai back to shore...*

≈⊱ *Choose your destiny* ⊰≈

To fight the Beast in the water, turn to **5**

To lure the Beast onto the land, turn to **14**

7

The trail of bubbles moves from pool
to pool. You have to run to keep up,
stumbling into patches of squelching mud
and forcing your way through prickly gorse
bushes. From behind, you can hear Tom,
Elenna and your animal friends panting for
breath.

The bubbles burst up in a pool buzzing
with flies, then in a pool of green water.
You pause, your eyes darting around to spot
where they appear next. Tom stands beside
you. Silver starts to lap at the filthy water,
but Elenna pulls him back.

"The bubbles have disappeared," you say.

There's a terrible roar, so loud that you
clamp your hands over your ears.

"It's coming from beneath us!" yells
Elenna.

The ground shakes. Clods of earth churn
up into the air. You're thrown aside, and
your stomach tightens in fear when you
see the creature burst out of the ground.

Its long, spiny body is armed with clawed feet, and its head tapers to a deadly point. Rows of eyes glitter with evil.

"Sanpao's Beast," you gasp.

The Beast opens its jaws to reveal long teeth. Drool loops between them and a waft of stinking breath makes you choke.

You reach for your sword. Panic rises in your throat when you realise that you lost your weapon when you fell. Desperately, you look round, but can't see anything other than a tangle of branches from a gorse bush.

Can I fight the Beast with one of those? you wonder. *Or is there time to find my sword?*

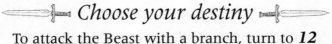 *Choose your destiny*

To attack the Beast with a branch, turn to **12**

To find your sword, turn to **31**

8

"Tom, Elenna," you call. "Keep Dredda distracted!"

Elenna launches a rain of arrows on the Beast, while Tom crashes his shield into her side.

You hold your sword steady. Dredda rears upwards and gives a ferocious roar, exposing the patch of raw flesh. *Now!*

You drive your blade upwards, straight into the Beast's weak spot. She gives a strangled, gurgling cry, and when you pull your sword out she stumbles backwards. Her body contorts, her tail whips back and forth. Her tough skin crumples and Dredda dissolves to ash. The Beast is defeated!

Elenna gives a cheer and Silver licks your hand.

"You did it!" cries Tom. "That was such a skilful attack."

Your chest swells with pride, but you know that your Quest is far from over.

Sanpao strides towards you. In his arms

is a large leather bundle.

"Dredda is gone," the Pirate King says, "but Sanpao remains."

He dumps the bundle on the ground, and the leather unrolls to reveal a stash of weapons. There are swords of every length, knives, an axe, a shield and a spear.

Sanpao steps towards you, his eyes glittering. "You defeated my Beast," he snarls, "and now I will take my revenge. Choose your weapon, and fight me in a duel!"

"Very well," you agree. You kneel down to inspect the weapons. Immediately, you see that the best are an axe with a handle made from bone, and a spear with a point cut from crystal. *But which one can help me defeat Sanpao?* you wonder.

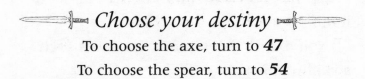 *Choose your destiny*

To choose the axe, turn to **47**

To choose the spear, turn to **54**

9

"Come on, Tom," you say. "Let's defeat this Beast!"

Dredda's head sways like a snake's. She knocks Tom aside with a huge paw, and raises it to stamp on his head...

"No!" you yell. A swing from your sword slices off one of the Beast's diamond claws. Howling, she writhes with anger, making the ground shake. It crumples like a broken eggshell. You, Tom and your horses plummet into the dark...

You land in an underground tunnel strewn with bones. Tom picks up a skull. "Looks like Dredda eats her prey here. And what's this?" he says.

You kneel beside him. There's a trail of marks on the ground. "Paw-prints," you reply. "But who made them – an escaped snack, or another Beast?"

You follow the trail along the tunnel, and after a few moments you hear a familiar howl.

"That's no Beast," Tom says, laughing. "It's Silver!"

You find the wolf and Elenna in a cavern. "I wondered where you were!" Elenna says with a smile. She pats Storm and Lightning.

The cavern is full of treasure. Heaps of jewels lie beside sacks of gold coins. There are pieces of armour and weapons too.

"Do you think it's Sanpao's loot?" Tom asks.

"I'm not sure. What's this doing here?" says Elenna, picking up a fish bone. "And this?" she adds, peeling some seaweed from a gold helmet.

Tom frowns. "Let's find out."

Before you leave, you just have time to take a piece of treasure with you. What do you choose?

Choose your destiny

To take a spear, turn to **24**

To take a crown, turn to **37**

10

You wade through the shallows by the lake shore. Ignoring the cold water that soaks up to your waist, you search desperately for Polkai.

"It's no good," says Elenna, a few paces away. "He's disappeared."

Silver splashes over and licks Elenna's hand. You wade over to where Lightning waits patiently. As you stroke her flank, you spot a strange footprint in the muddy sand. You kneel down for a better look. There's actually a trail of prints, each with its toes joined strangely together.

Webbed feet, you think. *These are Polkai's prints!*

You yell for Elenna, and follow the trail past a stream of bubbling rapids. They lead to a marsh. You place one foot into the soupy water then hurriedly withdraw it – the water sucks at your flesh.

Choose your destiny

To make your way down the rapids, turn to **2**

To go across the marsh, turn to **46**

11

"You can come with us," you say to the girl. "We'll do our best to protect you."

You lead Lightning down the path. Tom and Storm are behind you, followed by the girl.

Tom shouts in surprise. "Hey!"

You look round. The girl is holding the cutlass to his throat, her cloak falling away to reveal a black tunic with Sanpao's skull symbol on it.

"Fools!" she says with a laugh. "The cutlass is mine. I'm a pirate!" She presses the blade against Tom's skin, releasing a thread of blood.

"Let him go," you demand through gritted teeth.

You draw your sword, but suddenly the ground swells upwards beneath your feet. A shower of earth and plants shoots into the air, knocking you backwards.

Through a tangle of creepers, you see that the girl has been buried beneath a heap of mud and rock. Tom emerges from the debris.

"What's happening?" he shouts.

⟫─── *Choose your destiny* ───⟪

To stay and find out what's going on, turn to **3**

To run from the shower of earth, turn to **25**

12

The Beast lunges towards you. You slam the branch into her gaping jaws, wedging them open. Her eyes roll in confusion and she tosses her head, trying to shake the branch free.

Elenna's arrow bounces off the Beast's spiny flank. Tom charges with his blade, but her long tail bats him aside.

You spot a gleam of metal beneath a gorse bush. It's your sword! But as you pick it up, you hear a voice. "Fool! That poxy weapon won't save you."

Through the tendrils of green mist steps Sanpao. His band of pirates follow.

The Pirate King throws back his head and gives a peal of cruel laughter. "Do you really think swords and arrows are enough to defeat my Beast, Dredda the Tunnelling Menace?"

With a crunching sound, Dredda's jaws clamp down on the branch, shattering it. She spits out a shower of splinters. You

duck as one the size of a dagger hurtles past your head.

"Dredda will grind up your bones like that branch," Sanpao boasts. His crew laugh.

"Don't be so sure," you tell him.

The Beast slams her bony head towards you. You dart away, and her skull smashes through a rock instead. As the Beast raises her head once more, you spot something –

a tiny patch of raw skin on the underside
of her jaw.

A weak spot, you realise with excitement.
But it's only the size of your thumbnail
– to strike it, you will need to use deadly
accuracy...

⊰⚔ *Choose your destiny* ⚔⊱

To attack Dredda's weak spot with your
sword, turn to **8**
To attack Dredda's weak spot with one of
Elenna's arrows, turn to **20**

13

You shake your head. "But I'm not good enough to duel with Sanpao."

Elenna's eyes widen. "What do you mean? You just defeated Dredda – why can't you fight Sanpao?"

"You and Tom are better warriors," you explain. "Tom, can't you fight him instead?"

He frowns with disappointment. "I thought you were a brave Quester," he says sadly.

"Enough of this jibber-jabbering!" Sanpao steps towards you, his lip curled in a sneer. He jabs a finger at your chest. "You're just a yellow-dog coward," he says. "And cowards don't deserve to duel with Sanpao!"

The Pirate King yanks the spear from the ground and plunges it into your heart. Searing pain shoots through your body. Darkness washes over you...

Your Quest has failed. Sanpao will destroy Avantia...

14

"Polkai!" you shout. "Look what I've found – it's the red gem that Sanpao stole!"

The Beast gives a furious roar. "That belongs to my master," he snarls. "Give it back!"

As Polkai wades towards the shore, Elenna lets loose an arrow. It whizzes past the Beast's head, scraping his fin. He gives an agonised cry.

"That's Polkai's weak spot," you whisper excitedly to your friends. On the shore of the lake are long, thin shells with serrated edges. You pass one to Tom and pick up another for yourself.

"Everyone aim for his fin," you say.

Elenna shoots another arrow, and you and Tom hurl the shells. They pierce the Shark-Man's fin and he slumps to his knees.

You draw your sword, ready to strike the final blow.

Polkai looks up at you. "Please," he gasps. "Don't kill me."

Choose your destiny

To spare the Beast his life, turn to *21*

To kill the Beast, turn to *52*

15

"Back to shore," you yell to Elenna.
"Now!"

You heave the oars through the water.
But the Beast is too fast, and swims in lazy
circles around your boat.

"Do you think you can escape Polkai
the Shark-Man?" he bellows. His voice
is familiar.

"He sounds like Sanpao," you gasp.

Polkai roars. "Do not speak of my
treacherous brother! He fed me to the
sharks, and now brings me back as a Beast
to do his bidding."

"You don't have to do what he says,"
Elenna protests.

"He has cursed me," replies Polkai.
"I have no choice."

He rams the side of the boat, tipping you
and Elenna into the icy ocean. You open
your mouth to cry out and water fills your
lungs.

Polkai swims beneath you. His fin slices

through your stomach and the water turns
red with blood.

*Your Quest has failed. Sanpao will
destroy Avantia...*

16

Your head feels like someone is stamping on it. Slowly, you open your eyes to see a face framed with shaggy hair hovering over you. It belongs to Tagus the Horse-Man. The Good Beast is kneeling on his four legs, and gives a cry of relief.

"He heard our call for help," Tom said. "Our enemy struck you on the head, but disappeared when Tagus came charging over."

You get to your feet, gingerly rubbing a bruise at the base of your skull. "Thanks, friend," you tell Tagus.

The Good Beast raises his arm, gesturing for you to follow. You and Tom climb onto your horses, and the air soon thunders with the sound of three sets of hooves. Tagus takes you across the Central Plains. You pass over long stretches of grassland, startling herds of wild cattle. The ground becomes hilly, then opens up to reveal a rocky headland

with a waterfall gushing over it.

"I've never seen this place before,"
says Tom.

You climb down from Lightning. Behind
the waterfall glow eerie orbs of light.
Tagus nods his head.

"He's telling us to go through there,"
you say. "But what's on the other side?"

Choose your destiny
To go through the waterfall, turn to **6**
To refuse to go through the waterfall, turn to **44**

17

Sanpao grins, showing his rotten teeth.
"So it's a fiery death for you," he says. "You
shall walk the plank over the volcano!"

The ship flies northeast. Before long you
can see the brooding peak of the Stonewin
Volcano. Molten lava spews from its crater.

"Once we're dead, Avantia is doomed,"
Elenna says sadly. "Sanpao will take over
the kingdom."

The ship stops above the volcano.

"Move it!" bellows Sanpao. With his
cutlass, he prods you towards the plank.
"You first," he barks.

You step onto the narrow strip of wood.
Lava swirls dizzyingly beneath you and the
heat blasts your skin.

"Wait!" you cry, as an idea comes to you.
"If you spare us, we'll join your crew. We
know so many of Avantia's secrets – we can
help you take all the treasure you want."

Sanpao strokes his chin. "So be it," he
agrees. "But first, you must pass my test…"

The ship moves away from the volcano. "We'll escape as soon as we can," you whisper to Tom and Elenna.

When the ship stops again, it sinks down into the centre of a village. A dam protects the houses from a churning river.

"This is your test," Sanpao says. "You must join our pirate raid!"

Cutlasses raised, the pirates swarm over the deck. You follow on Lightning, with Tom and Elenna on Storm. A bottle drops from Sanpao's pocket as he slashes his blade at the terrified villagers. You lean down to pick it up.

We've got to stop this raid, you think. *But how?*

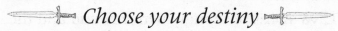 *Choose your destiny*

To use the bottle dropped by Sanpao, turn to **35**

To breach the dam so the river carries away the pirates, turn to **40**

18

"This way, Lightning," you say, coaxing your horse down the right-hand path. She gives a nervous whinny. *She can sense something she doesn't like*, you think. *What could it be?*

Storm seems nervous too. Tom pats his flank, murmuring, "Good boy. We've got to keep going to defeat the pirates."

The path is dotted with more mounds of upturned soil. There are pillars of earth, too, taller than the horses, and baked dry in the sun. They're covered in holes that make you imagine there's a network of tunnels inside.

"What are they?" you wonder as Lightning trots by an enormous pillar with dust spewing from the top.

The next moment, Lightning gives a terrified neigh. She rears up on her back legs, tipping you onto the ground. Scrambling to your feet, you see that a gigantic ant has its jaws clamped to her left foreleg. The insect is the size of your hand and its body glows red.

"Hold still, girl," you tell your horse, and pierce the ant with your sword. Red slime drips from it and the insect falls to the ground. "There, it's gone," you say.

"But its friends are here now," gulps Tom. "Those pillars are ant nests!"

Hundreds of ants swarm out from the holes in the pillars. Their red bodies glow like burning coals, and when they surge over a patch of grass, it bursts into flame.

"Fire ants!" you yell.

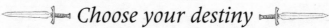

Choose your destiny

To make for higher ground to try to escape
the ants, turn to **42**
To try to smash the ants with your shield,
turn to **55**

19

"Ouch!" you mutter. The forest is buzzing with insects, and you rub a large bite on the side of your neck. Lightning swats the flies away with her tail.

At the edge of the forest, you raise a finger to your lips. The battling Beasts are so close that you can feel the ground tremble with the force of their punches and kicks.

The shark-Beast swings around so that his serrated fin slices across Arcta's arm. A clump of fur falls away and Arcta roars in pain.

"Prepare to be destroyed," the Beast snarls. "None can defeat Polkai!" He draws back, ready to spring at the Mountain Giant.

This is your chance. "Now!" you yell.

Elenna immediately lets loose an arrow. It whizzes straight through Polkai's empty ribcage, making him stagger in surprise. Raising your sword, you sprint out from the trees, and swing it at Polkai's fin.

But the Beast dodges aside before your

blow can fall. With a roar of anger, he dives into the lake. "I won't forget this," he hisses. Only his fin is visible as he swims away.

Arcta raises a hairy arm in thanks, then disappears into the forest.

"We should go after Polkai," says Elenna. "He might lead us to the Fire Stone."

But as she speaks, the sky darkens. The

hulking mass of the flying pirate ship comes into view, blocking the sunlight.

What do we do now? you ask yourself.

Choose your destiny

To go after Polkai, turn to **10**

To go after the Pirate Ship, turn to **33**

"Elenna," you call. "Pass me one of your arrows!"

She reaches into her quiver and tosses an arrow over to you.

Tom is slashing at the Beast with his sword. Dredda's skin is so tough that his blade just leaves faint scratches, but the Beast is furious. She snaps at Tom with her teeth, her eyes swivelling to follow his movements.

She's not looking at me, you think. You seize your opportunity and dart towards the Beast. Dodging her thrashing tail, you crouch by her side. Tom swings another blow and she bellows with anger – exposing the patch of raw flesh.

You slam the arrow into it. Dredda gives a roar of shock and you let go, leaving the arrow embedded in her skull. The Beast slumps to the ground, her eyes rolling back. Her tail twitches and then she lies completely still.

Relief hits you like a wave. "She's gone!"

Grinning, Tom slaps you on the back. Elenna pulls you into a hug. "Well done!" she says.

Dredda's huge body turns grey then crumbles into ash. It drifts away on the breeze.

"How dare you!" snarls Sanpao. "No one defeats my Beast and gets away with it!"

He strides up to you. In Sanpao's hands are two spears with crystal points. He rams one into the ground beside your feet.

"Fight me in a duel," he challenges you. "Then we'll find out who the true victor is!"

You glance at Tom and Elenna. Are you the best warrior to fight Sanpao? Or should you ask one of your friends to face him instead?

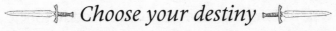 *Choose your destiny*

To ask Tom or Elenna to fight Sanpao, turn to **13**

To fight Sanpao yourself, turn to **54**

21

You lower your sword and stretch out a hand to the wretched Beast. He grips it, and as you help Polkai stand you notice how human his eyes seem.

"Polkai," you ask. "Will you tell us your story?"

The Beast nods. "I have waited a long time to reveal the truth about myself – and about Sanpao. He is my brother."

You can hardly believe Polkai's words. Elenna gasps in shock.

"Many years ago," Polkai explains, "it was not Sanpao who was King of the Pirates, but me. I was a man then. My crew would have followed me to the end of the known realms. We only stole from those who were evil, and gave our bounty to the needy. Perhaps you know Malvel, the Dark Wizard?"

Tom nods. "Yes! He's an old enemy of ours."

"We looted his treasure room once,"

Polkai says. "But Sanpao was jealous of my success. He used his cunning words to turn the crew against me. In the end, he forced me to walk the plank."

Your fists clench with anger. "Sanpao murdered his own brother," you mutter.

Polkai sighs. "If only he had murdered me – my fate was far worse. He cursed my body so that I fused with the sharks that swam the waters. I became a Beast under his command." His eyes suddenly shine. "But when you defeated me, you broke Sanpao's curse. I'm free!"

"Then tell us how to overcome your brother," you ask.

"Gladly," Polkai agrees. "But on one condition – that you let me fight alongside you."

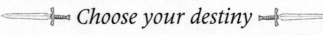 *Choose your destiny*

To let Polkai fight alongside you, turn to **30**

To refuse to let Polkai fight alongside you, turn to **53**

22

The blade of your sword is green from
the creepers you've sliced through.

"Let's get out of here," you say, "and
find Sanpao's Beasts!"

Soon you and Tom are riding across
the Central Plains. The ground shudders,
making Lightning stumble. Tom frowns.
"It feels like an earthquake," he says.

The path slopes down between steep,
narrow walls of rock. It twists and turns
like a snake.

Whoosh! There's an explosion ahead of
you. Through the shower of rocks and
earth, you see a terrible Beast. Her long,
muscular body emerges out of the ground,
powered by diamond-clawed feet. Her head
narrows to a tapered skull, and her wide
jaws reveal broad, flat teeth. *They look like
they could grind through bone*, you think.

"Looks like we've found one of the
Beasts, anyway," says Tom grimly.

From the path behind you echoes a voice

singing a jaunty tune. *"With a yo-ho-ho, and a hee-hee-hee, we take to Avantia's seas..."* To your amazement, a girl saunters round a bend in the rock walls. Long red hair swirls around her shoulders. At her belt hangs a whip, and her black tunic bears Sanpao's skull symbol.

"She's a pirate!" gasps Tom.

The girl rolls her eyes. "You don't say," she scoffs. "I thought you were supposed to be clever."

She takes a flask from her pocket and pulls out the cork.

"What's that?" you ask.

"Travel grog," she replies. "You can drink it, and magically appear on our pirate ship. Or you can stay here and make friends with Dredda the Tunnelling Menace..."

Choose your destiny

To stay and fight Dredda, turn to **9**

To drink the grog and go to the pirate ship, turn to **56**

23

Tom runs to help the villagers while you and Elenna wait for the pirate ship to land. It's made from black wood and topped with blood-red sails. Its flag bears the same skull symbol that is tattooed on the pirates' arms.

"There could be hordes of pirates on board," you say. Your sword is gripped tightly in your hand and Elenna has an arrow notched in her bow.

When the ship is just a hand's breadth above the ground, it shudders and stops. From somewhere on board comes a bellow of laughter. Just one man leaps out – but the sight of him makes fear coil inside your stomach.

He's the tallest man you've ever seen. A black jerkin stretches across his broad chest and tattoos cover his thick arms. His face is heavily scarred, with the left eye held partially shut by a lump of burnt flesh. Silver darts gleam in his long plait of hair.

"Look who's here," he bellows. "It's

my old friend, Elenna."

"I'm not your friend," Elenna snaps. At her feet, Silver growls.

The man turns to you. "Since Elenna's forgotten her manners, allow me to introduce myself. I'm Sanpao, the Pirate King – and you, young Quester, are in my way."

In a flash, Sanpao pulls a cutlass from his belt and swings it towards you. You're forced to spring aside.

The Pirate King marches to a pillar at the centre of the village square. Using the tip of his cutlass, he prises out the red gem that's set into the stone.

"No!" cries an old woman in a green shawl. She dashes forwards and tugs at Sanpao's sleeve.

He knocks her aside and the gem falls into his palm. He puts it in his trouser pocket. "Men!" Sanpao yells. "We've emptied this poxy village of treasure. All aboard!"

The pirates gather up their loot and clamber onto the ship. Sanpao stands on the ship railings, his cutlass raised.

"We plunder wherever we please," he warns you and Elenna. "Don't even think about coming after us – or my two Beasts will destroy you as quick as cannon-fire."

The ship soars up and away, taking a westward course. To your surprise, the villagers seem to be ignoring their ruined homes. Instead, they're gathered around the stone pillar.

There must have been something special about that gem, you think.

You see that the old woman in the green shawl has tears in her eyes. "Please help us," she says. "The gem is called the Fire Stone. It has magical healing powers. Without it, our people will fall ill. We could all die."

"The pirates didn't seem to know about the Fire Stone's power," you say. "Don't worry – we'll get it back before they find out."

Tom comes over and you decide what to do. Tom will scour the Central Plains for Sanpao's Beasts, while you and Elenna head towards the Western Ocean.

"The pirate ship was heading that way," you point out.

You wave goodbye to Tom, then head back down the mountain. But Silver is sniffing a patch of undergrowth. With a bark, he trots off.

"Looks like he's found a trail," says Elenna.

⟨══╼ *Choose your destiny* ╾══⟩
To follow Silver, turn to **4**
To continue to the Western Ocean, turn to **41**

24

Holding the spear, you walk along the tunnel. Some sections are so dark that you have to feel your way along the wall. Silver's fur brushes your leg as he pads ahead.

"Silver," Elenna calls. "Don't run off."

The wolf gives a bark – which turns into a yelp of pain.

"He's being attacked!" cries Tom.

In the dim light, you can see something long wrapped around Silver's front leg. His teeth flash as he bites into it, but the creature doesn't budge.

You pull its tail – and shudder. The creature's slimy to the touch, like a giant slug. Then you remember the spear. "Elenna, keep Silver still."

Careful not to let the spear hurt Silver, you stab it into the coils of flesh. A stench like rotten eggs fills the tunnel, and then the creature falls away, lifeless.

"Thank you!" cries Elenna. Silver gives you a grateful lick.

"Well done," sneers a voice you don't recognise.

It's coming from above. You stare upwards, trying to spot the speaker. Elenna places an arrow to her bow.

"But how will you fare against a more deadly foe?" the voice continues. "Such as I, Polkai the Shark-Man?"

The Beast drops down from the shadows.

He lands on Tom, pinning him to the ground. Polkai's body is a human skeleton, and on the back of his skull you can see the outline of a shark's fin. In his webbed hand is a cutlass.

"Get back!" you order the Beast, swinging your sword at his ribcage. It passes harmlessly between his bones, but Elenna's arrow makes a tear in Polkai's fin. He shrieks with pain and Tom wriggles free.

"His fin's his weak point," you pant. "Attack!"

─────◆── *Choose your destiny* ──◆─────
To attack Polkai's fin yourself, turn to **27**
To keep Polkai occupied so Tom and Elenna can attack his fin, turn to **32**

25

The creepers' leaves feel like knives across your palms as you tear them from your body. Jumping up, you yell to Tom. "Let's go!"

You scramble onto Lightning's back and urge her across the Central Plains. Storm's hooves thunder as he and Tom follow.

A strong wind howls in your ears. Tom yells something but you can't make out his words. Instead, you look in the direction of his outstretched arm. On the horizon is a Beast – it has a man's head and torso, and a horse's body and legs. Tagus the Horse-Man!

Thump! Something strikes you on the back of the head and you fall from Lightning's back. To your horror, a pirate is standing over you, a club in his hand. Tom is also slumped on the ground.

"Come aboard our ship, you scurvy

scum," the pirate growls. "Sanpao wants a word with you..."

To call for Tagus's help, turn to **16**
To go on board the pirate ship, turn to **56**

26

"Help me! Please!" Elenna begs.

You ignore her and swim for the shore. But as soon as your foot touches the bank, a thick tentacle snares your ankle. The tentacle belongs to a gigantic jellyfish. It rises out of the water.

You fumble for your sword, but another tentacle shoots out and wrenches your weapon away. Then the jellyfish reels you into the pool.

"No!" yells Elenna. She manages to reach an arrow from her quiver and slashes at the tentacles that grip her. She takes aim at the giant jellyfish too.

She's trying to save me, you think. *I don't deserve her help...*

It's your final thought. A tentacle squeezes your neck and the world turns black.

Your Quest has failed. Sanpao will destroy Avantia...

27

You and Polkai circle each other. The
Beast carefully keeps his back from
you, so you can't reach his fin. Tom
and Elenna wait. You can see the worry
in their eyes. The animals stand in the
shadows, giving you an idea.

"You'll never catch me," you say, and
jump into a patch of darkness. Polkai
springs after you, swinging his cutlass.
But you've already moved away. You slip
out of the shadows and creep behind him
– slicing your sword into his fin.

Polkai gives a bloodcurdling cry. He tries to stagger towards you, but collapses to the ground.

"I was not always like this," the Beast gasps. "Once, I was a man. Will you grant me mercy – so I can feel human again?"

Choose your destiny

To grant Polkai mercy, turn to **21**

To refuse Polkai's request, turn to **52**

28

"He's gone – for now," you say, as Polkai disappears into the distance. But you can't see Uncle Leo's fishing village anywhere.

"We must have drifted," says Elenna. "Let's row to shore and find our bearings."

You move swiftly through the water. As you reach land, you're greeted by excited howls and a neigh.

"Silver and Lightning!" you say. "They must have been watching our boat and followed it along the shore."

Your faithful animals stay nearby as you draw into an inlet. The water is as clear as a mirror – with Sanpao's ship reflected in its surface.

With a gasp, you look up to see that the pirate ship is over your head. Two long chains with hooks drop over the side and latch onto your fishing boat. The chains crank upwards again, and with a jerk your boat is lifted out of the water.

"They're taking us on board!" you cry.

Choose your destiny

To jump out of the boat, turn to **2**

To let the pirate pull you up to their ship,
turn to **56**

29

You and Tom guide your horses down the left-hand path. The cutlass is lying beside a dense thorn bush, and you jump to the ground to pick it up. The hilt is made from green metal and the blade is scratched, as if it's been used in many battles.

There's a rustling sound from behind the thorn bush.

"That must be the pirate this cutlass belongs to," you mutter. Tom climbs down from Storm's back and you both draw your swords. Quietly, you move towards the bush.

"There he is," you whisper. A figure is crouched among the thorny branches, draped in a long green cloak. You can't see his face. *What a coward*, you think.

Lunging into the bush, you grab a green-cloaked shoulder. "Come out and fight, pirate!"

You gasp as the cloak falls away to reveal a girl about your age. She has long red hair and her blue eyes are filled with tears.

"I'm sorry," you say, releasing her. "I – er – we thought you were a pirate."

"Have they left my village yet?" the girl asks, her hands clasped together. "I'm so scared they'll come back. Please – can I travel with you?"

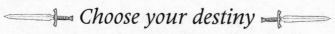 *Choose your destiny*

To let the girl travel with you, turn to **11**

To refuse to let the girl travel with you, turn to **51**

30

"Fight Sanpao with us," you say to Polkai.

The Shark-Man nods. His body glows with a strange, golden light, and to your amazement the Beast disappears. In his place stands a muscular man with long blond hair. He holds a silver cutlass.

"Polkai," Elenna breathes.

"Yes," he says. "By your brave deeds you have restored me." He takes a vial of silver liquid from his pocket and removes the cork. "Here – drink this. It will take us to my brother. To defeat him, we must harness the power of his crew..."

The magical liquid slides down your throat. With a brilliant flash, you and your friends appear on the deck of the pirate ship. Murmurs of amazement ripple through the crew. "P-Polkai?" a pirate stammers. "We thought you were dead."

The blood drains from Sanpao's face. "Don't just stand there," he orders his men. "Throw these fools overboard. Attack!"

But none of the pirates move. Polkai raises his cutlass and a silver light shines from the blade. It falls over the crew and they rub their eyes, as if woken from a dream.

Tom grins. "The power Sanpao had over them is gone. They're Polkai's crew now!"

The pirates crowd around Polkai. "Our King is back!" one of them cries. Cheers fill

the ship. At Polkai's command, the crew drag Sanpao into a cell, slam the door shut and draw the bolts. "Let's make him walk the plank later," suggests one of the crew. "Just like he made Polkai do."

Sanpao rattles the bars of the cell. "You poxy dogs! You wouldn't dare!"

You whisper an idea to Polkai and he nods in agreement. Then you step towards Sanpao. "Polkai will spare you the plank – but only if you hand over the red gem."

Sanpao scowls, but he takes the Fire Stone from his pocket and tosses it through the bars. It rolls across the deck. The air shimmers, and a bearded man in flowing robes appears. He stoops to pick up the Fire Stone.

"Aduro!" you cry.

The Good Wizard smiles. "Congratulations! Your Quest is won. I will take the Fire Stone back to the village – while you start the celebrations!"

To celebrate your victory, turn to **50**

31

You scramble to your feet. Your sword is lying in a clump of reeds, half-hidden in the green mist. You hurry towards it. But before you can pick the sword up, a hand extends through the mist and seizes it.

"Lost something?" sneers a voice. Sanpao steps into view, surrounded by his gang of pirates. "I see you've met my Beast, Dredda the Tunnelling Menace."

Dredda roars as if greeting her master. She slashes at Tom with one of her clawed feet, and he wards off her blow with his shield.

Sanpao grins. "Watching Dredda destroy you will be better than a spree of pillaging. Here," he says, handing you your sword. "I want the fun to last as long as possible."

You grip your weapon fiercely. "You're going to be disappointed, Sanpao. Giving me back my weapon is the greatest mistake you'll ever make."

With a yell, you charge at the Beast.

But your blade bounces off her thick hide. Elenna looses an arrow, but Dredda catches it between her teeth, grinding the shaft to dust.

The Beast swings her head at you like a gigantic club. You roll over, away from her blow – and catch sight of a tiny soft spot on the underside of her jaw.

Her skin's too tough to pierce anywhere else, you think. *If I can strike Dredda there, maybe she'll be defeated!*

Your blow will need to be accurate. Should you trust your sword skills or ask Elenna for one of her arrows?

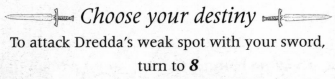 *Choose your destiny*

To attack Dredda's weak spot with your sword, turn to **8**

To attack Dredda's weak spot with one of Elenna's arrows, turn to **20**

32

You look straight into the Beast's empty eye
sockets. "Let's fight!"

With a snarl, Polkai launches at you. You
meet his cutlass with your sword, swinging
it down to make Polkai stagger sideways.

"Tom, Elenna," you call. "Get his fin!"

Her eyes narrowed, Elenna releases her
shot. The arrow tip scratches the Beast's fin
and he winces with pain.

"It'll take more than that to defeat me," Polkai snarls, but his voice trembles.

You slam your sword into his skull, backing the Beast towards Tom. He runs the fin through with his sword, while Elenna pierces it with arrow after arrow. Polkai drops to his knees.

"One more blow will destroy him forever," says Tom.

But Polkai looks up at you. "I was human once. Will you show me mercy?"

Choose your destiny

To show Polkai mercy, turn to **21**

To destroy Polkai forever, turn to **52**

33

Boooom! Boooom!

The sound is so loud that it blasts thoughts of Polkai from your head. Lightning whinnies in fright and Silver hides behind Elenna's legs.

"It's cannon-fire," says Elenna grimly, pointing to the sky.

The pirate ship sinks down through the clouds. Its blood-red sails billow and you can make out pirates scurrying on deck to reload the cannons.

BOOOOOOM!

A cannonball crashes into the ground at your feet, sending up a shower of earth.

"They're firing at us," you cry. "Run!"

You and Elenna scramble onto Lightning. You urge her into a gallop, Silver sprinting behind.

But the ground soon becomes a spongy marsh, sucking at your horse's hooves. The pirate ship moves to hover right over your head.

"Are you too lily-livered to stay and fight?" Sanpao yells down.

Choose your destiny

To continue across the marsh, turn to **46**

To fight Sanpao, turn to **56**

34

"Hand it over, my pretty!" a pirate snarls
to a frightened young woman. He grabs
her hand and prises a ring from her finger.

With a yell, you charge. You ram the
pirate's arm with the hilt of your sword,
and with a yelp he lets go of the woman.

"Oh, thank you!" she gasps.

The pirate ship is now hovering just
above the ground. A gigantic man with a
heavily scarred face leaps out. In his hand
glints a cutlass with a serrated edge. The
man grins as his gaze flickers over the
cowering villagers.

"I know him," Tom says. "He's Sanpao
the Pirate King."

Sanpao makes his way to a pillar in
the centre of the village square, shoving
protesting villagers aside. With the tip of his
cutlass, he knocks free the red gem set at
the top of the pillar, then drops it into his
trouser pocket.

"Crew!" Sanpao yells. The pirates stop

attacking the villagers and turn towards
him. "This place is hardly worth looting."
He spits on the ground. "Let's find some
real treasure. All aboard!"

Their pockets bulging with stolen loot,

the pirate crew and Sanpao climb onto the ship. Its blood-red sails billow and it takes off. Soon, it's out of sight among the clouds.

An old man sinks to the ground in front of the pillar. The space that held the red gem looks like an empty eye socket. "It's gone," the old man sobs. "We're doomed!"

You exchange puzzled glances with Tom and Elenna. *What's so special about that gem?*

As if in response to your thoughts, the air in front of you shimmers. An elderly man with a long beard appears. It's Aduro, the Good Wizard of Avantia!

"Greetings, brave Questers," he says. His forehead is creased with worry.

"Aduro, what is it?" you ask. "Is it to do with the red gem?"

The wizard nods. "It's called the Fire Stone. It protects the village from sickness," he explains. "Without it, disease will spread. The people will die."

Elenna's eyes are wide with alarm. "Then we've got to get it back from Sanpao," she declares.

"It won't be easy," Aduro says. "Sanpao has created two new Beasts to guard his stolen treasure. My magic cannot tell what form these Beasts have taken, but I do know that one Beast is of the land, and the other dwells in water."

You grit your teeth in determination. "Then we'll split up," you say. "Tom and I will search the land, while Elenna goes to the Western Ocean."

Aduro starts to fade. "You have one advantage," he tells you. "Sanpao doesn't know the power of the Fire Stone. He thinks it's just an ordinary jewel. You must get it back before he finds out..."

The wizard disappears. You look towards the villagers for the last time. Many are weeping, while others hang their heads in despair. Then Elenna and Silver leave for the ocean, and you and Tom set off towards the Central Plains.

You guide your horses along a narrow path. It isn't long before it splits in two. Down the right fork is a huge mound of disturbed soil, like a giant molehill.

Lying in the left fork is a pirate cutlass.
"Which way?" Tom asks.

Choose your destiny

To take the right fork, turn to **18**

To take the left fork, turn to **29**

35

You snatch up the bottle. An orange gas swirls inside.

What does this do? you wonder.

As if in answer, a wise voice fills your head. It's Aduro!

Trust the magic of the potion, the Good Wizard tells you. *It will aid whoever opens the bottle.*

You pull out the cork. The gas pours from the top and swirls in the air to form the shape of a hand. It swoops towards a pirate robbing an old woman of her bracelet, and as soon as it touches him, he disappears. Then it flies to a pirate filling his pockets with coins, and he vanishes as well.

"Run!" a pirate yells. But they can't move quickly enough. The hand makes pirate after pirate disappear.

The villagers cheer. "They've gone!" shouts Tom.

"Not quite," says a voice heavy with anger. It's Sanpao. He stands on the deck of his ship, his cutlass held aloft. "That magic isn't powerful enough to defeat the Pirate King," he snarls. "And now you will be punished. Dredda – destroy these meddling Questers!"

At Sanpao's command, the village square rips apart and a Beast bursts up from the earth. Dredda rams her skull towards you. Grabbing a shovel that leans against a wall, you swing it at her, but the Beast's teeth clamp down onto it. To your horror, she bites through the metal handle as easily as a piece of bread.

But you've spotted something: a patch of raw skin underneath her jaw. *Her hide's tough everywhere else*, you think. *That's her weak spot!*

But how should you attack it?

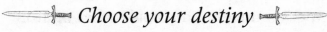 *Choose your destiny*

To attack Dredda's weak spot with your sword, turn to **8**

To attack Dredda's weak spot with one of Elenna's arrows, turn to **20**

36

The boat sways from side to side. You stand with your feet apart to keep your balance. "I'm not afraid," you tell the Beast. Elenna fixes an arrow to her bow.

The Beast roars, showing its rows of jagged teeth. "Foolish Questers! You shall feel the wrath of Polkai the Shark Man."

Polkai dives beneath the water once more. Only his fin is visible as he circles the boat. Elenna leans over the edge, trying to train her arrow on him. "He's too fast to get a clear shot," she mutters.

The boat suddenly lurches to the side. You lose your balance, and topple onto your hands and knees. "He's trying to make us capsize!" you yell.

With a huge splash, Polkai rises up from the water, his skull-face grinning. Then he swims across the surface of the ocean, towards the shore.

"After him!" yells Elenna, seizing an oar. You heave the oars through the water.

To your surprise, you soon gain on the
Beast. "It's as if he wants us to follow," you
say. "Maybe he's leading us into a trap."

 *Choose your destiny*

To carry on chasing Polkai, turn to **10**

To stop chasing Polkai, turn to **28**

37

Clutching the crown, you follow your friends out of the cavern and down the tunnel. The ground becomes damp and dotted with pools of water. Every so often you pass more fronds of seaweed.

Silver pauses by a stretch of shadow, his hackles raised. He growls low in his throat.

"What is it, boy?" Elenna whispers.

A figure emerges from the shadows. It has a skull for a face, and black rags hang from its empty ribcage. On its back is a shark's fin, and in its webbed hand it carries a cutlass.

"A Beast!" Tom gasps.

"I am Polkai the Shark-Man," the Beast snarls. "And that's my crown!"

You glance down at it. *So that's why the treasure had seaweed on it*, you think. *It belongs to this Beast.*

Polkai steps towards you. "Give it back," he demands.

"Alright," you agree. "But in return, you

must tell us where the Fire Stone is."

Polkai snatches the crown. "I won't tell you anything," he sneers, and points his cutlass at your throat. "Now you shall pay for stealing my treasure!"

Elenna lets fly an arrow that goes straight through the Beast's ribcage. It gives you the chance to back away from Polkai's blade. You draw your sword, looking your enemy up and down for weak spots. *How do you attack a skeleton?* you wonder.

Tom must be thinking the same thing. "The only weak part of him is the fin," Tom says. "Aim for that!"

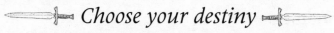

Choose your destiny

To attack Polkai's fin yourself, turn to **27**

To keep Polkai occupied so Tom and Elenna can attack his fin, turn to **32**

38

"Elenna's right," you say, and point to a tree growing beside one of the stagnant pools. "Let's climb up there and see where the bubbles are heading."

Silver and the two horses wait on a patch of mossy rock. Spines the size of your hand grow all over the tree, and you use them as rungs to help you climb.

When you're among the branches, you peer out at the marsh. Through shreds of green mist, you see a cluster of bubbles surface in one of the pools, and then another.

Elenna and Tom sit on the branch beside you. "They're heading west," says Tom.

"And now they're changing direction," Elenna says.

Your blood runs cold as you realise that the bubbles are heading straight towards your tree. "Get down – quick!" you yell.

But it's too late. A Beast erupts from the water and slams into the trunk. You catch

sight of a snake-like body, gaping jaws
and glittering eyes. Then, with a terrible
shudder, the tree collapses, tossing you to
the ground.

You land in a clump of reeds. Your fingers
reach for your sword but the fall has flung
it away. A splintered branch lies beside you.

Choose your destiny

To attack the Beast with the branch, turn to **12**

To find your sword, turn to **31**

39

When you, Tom and Elenna ride into the mountain village where your Quest began, you're immediately surrounded by a throng of people.

"Did you find it?" calls a woman holding a broom.

"Are the pirates here?" cries a man wearing a blacksmith's apron.

The old woman in the green shawl raises her hand. "Give our friends time to answer!"

You climb down from Lightning and present her with the Fire Stone. "Sanpao and his crew have gone," you say. "Avantia is safe!"

Cheers erupt throughout the crowd. The blacksmith carefully fixes the Fire Stone back into the stone pillar and you put your fingers to your lips, giving a whistle of celebration.

Elenna grins. "Our Quest has succeeded!"

"And you'll soon become a Knight of

Avantia," Tom says to you.

With your friends by your side and courage in your heart, you're ready for whatever adventures lie ahead.

The End

40

"Warn the villagers to get indoors," you yell to Tom and Elenna. "I'll burst the dam!"

"Good luck," calls Tom. He and Elenna rush over to a group of children, urging them into one of the houses.

You scramble up the rock face that leads to the dam. Soon, you're high above the village. The marauding pirates seem as tiny as wooden figurines. The dam is constructed from logs bound together with rope. Behind it gushes the river.

"Here goes," you mutter.

You wind your arm through a length of vine that grows alongside the dam, then slash at the ropes with your sword. As they tear, the logs shift. They tumble away down the rock face and the river is released.

A great torrent of water swirls down. It pours over you, but the vine stops you from being swept away. Below, the water rushes into the pirates. Many are carried out of the village, while only a few manage to scramble on board their ship.

When the waters clear, you climb back down. Tom, Elenna and your animal friends emerge from one of the houses. The villagers step outside too.

"You saved us," cries one woman. "Thank you!"

Sanpao stands bedraggled on the deck of his ship. "You will pay for this," he snarls. "Feel the wrath of Dredda!"

The sodden ground trembles. With a ferocious roar, the Beast erupts out of the earth. She writhes in anger, swinging at you with her bony skull.

You dodge her blow, and notice a soft patch of skin on the underside of her jaw. A weak spot! But how should you attack it?

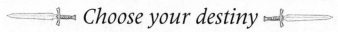 *Choose your destiny*

To attack with your sword, turn to **8**

To attack with one of Elenna's arrows, turn to **20**

41

The Western Ocean stretches out before you like a carpet of glittering blue. Elenna sits behind you on Lightning, while Silver pads ahead.

Elenna points towards a cluster of huts on the shore. "That's where my Uncle Leo lives. Maybe he's seen Sanpao – or his Beasts."

You turn Lightning towards the village. Fishing boats bob on the water, and a man is dragging a net heavy with fish onto the beach.

"Uncle Leo!" Elenna cries. She leaps down from the saddle and runs to hug him.

"What are you two doing here?" Leo asks with a grin. "Sorry – you three," he adds, patting Silver.

You decide not to tell Leo about your Quest – there's no point worrying him. "We just want some sea air," you say. "Can we borrow your boat?"

Uncle Leo agrees. Leaving Silver and

Lightning on the beach, you and Elenna row out to sea. You scan the horizon for any sign of the pirate ship.

"Sanpao didn't know how powerful the Fire Stone is, did he?" you say.

But Elenna doesn't reply. Instead, she points a shaking finger at something.

You turn to see a Beast rising out of the water. Its face is a human skull, but its jaws open to reveal rows of shark's teeth. Tattered black rags hang from its skeletal body, which has patches of grey shark's skin. The Beast's webbed hands are clawed flippers and a fin with a jagged edge grows from its back.

You must decide what to do – and quickly...

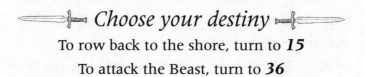 *Choose your destiny*

To row back to the shore, turn to **15**

To attack the Beast, turn to **36**

42

The carpet of fiery ants swarms over the path. Looking desperately around, you spot a steep hill with a tree at the top.

"This way!" you yell, hoping that the ants won't follow.

Tom dashes ahead. The horse's hooves skitter as they scramble up the slope, and you can see the whites of Lightning's frightened eyes.

A stabbing pain grips your ankle. One of the ants has sunk its jaws into your flesh. Grabbing a stone, you smash the huge insect, and it falls away in a smear of red slime.

"Hurry!" shouts Tom. He's already at the top of the hill, standing under the tree. The horses are beside him.

With a final leap over a boulder, you get there too. Below, the ants swarm down the path.

"We're safe," you pant.

A creeper hanging from the tree's

branches trails around your shoulder. You flick it away, but the creeper slides around your neck like a snake.

"Hey!" you yell.

More creepers drop down. They wrap around your arms and legs, and drag you and Tom up into the branches. You struggle as they mesh together to form a net – with you and Tom inside.

"We're trapped!" Tom gasps.

A dark shape moves across the sky. It's Sanpao's ship! The pirates let down a hook on the end of a chain. You realise what's about to happen – the pirates will hoist you up into their ship!

⟶⊱ *Choose your destiny* ⊰⟵
To escape from the net, turn to **22**
To let the pirates pull you up to their ship,
turn to **56**

43

"Hold on, Elenna!" you shout. "I'm going to save you!"

You swim towards her, dodging round the clusters of drifting jellyfish. You can see the creature that's trapped your friend. Its quivering body bobs beside her and its tentacles are wrapped around her arm. She splutters, struggling to keep her head above the surface.

Treading water, you aim your sword at the creature's heart. But it flicks its tentacles and moves away, dragging Elenna with it. You try again but it slides past your blow, to a stretch of the pool by a pillar studded with purple gems. With a hiss, the jellyfish scoots away from the colourful stones.

"I know how to get rid of it!" you shout. You swim towards the pillar. With the hilt of your sword, you chip away a chunk of purple gemstone. Then you swim towards Elenna.

"Let her go," you say, pressing the gem

against the jellyfish's body. With a terrible hiss, it unravels its tentacles from Elenna's arm.

"Thanks," she gasps. You drag her towards the shore and onto dry land. "I'm fine," she says, flexing her arm. "Those gems must be magical – like the Fire Stone."

Silver gives his mistress a relieved lick and you make your way through a patch of woodland. Cries of fear carry through the trees and you quicken your pace. When you emerge from the woods, you see a village ahead with a huge ship in the middle of it.

"Sanpao's ship," you say. "His crew are attacking another village!"

Some of the pirates set fire to houses, while others chase startled sheep and smash carts. You draw you sword, but before you can run to the villagers' aid, Elenna grabs your arm.

"There's someone else in the woods," she whispers. "Listen!"

Sure enough, a twig snaps and leaves

rustle. A figure steps into view.

"Tom!" you and Elenna both shout.
Storm follows him out from the trees.

You hug each other, then turn back
towards the village.

"I've been scouting ways to get rid of
the pirates," Tom says. He takes a bottle
of green liquid from Storm's saddlebag.
"Sanpao dropped this. It's magical. I think
it could help us." Then he points towards
a dam beside the village, which holds back
a swirling river. "Or we could flush the
pirates away."

Choose your destiny

To see what the bottle will do, turn to **35**
To breach the dam, turn to **40**

44

"I'm not going through that waterfall,"
you insist. "It looks dangerous."

Tom looks puzzled. "But we've got to
complete our Beast Quest," he says, "no
matter how dangerous it is."

You sit down in a patch of spongy
moss. "Go ahead," you tell Tom. "I'll wait
here."

While Tom wades through the pool at
the base of the waterfall. Tagus eyes you
coldly. With a snort of disgust, the Good
Beast canters away.

Something is tickling your arm. It's a
tiny green spider. With a start, you realise
that more spiders are climbing over you.
The patch of moss is covered with their
webs.

"I'm sitting on a spider nest," you
mutter – then gasp with pain. A spider
the size of your hand has sunk its fangs
into your wrist.

Immediately, your arm turns green.

Your throat swells and you can't call for help. Helplessly, you understand that death awaits...

Your Quest has failed. Sanpao will destroy Avantia...

45

"It's no ordinary gem," you boast. "It's called the Fire Stone and it's got special protective powers."

Tom and Elenna gape at you in horror. "Never tell secrets to Avantia's enemies!" Elenna shouts angrily.

You ignore them and look at Sanpao, hoping that he'll be full of envy at how clever you are. But the Pirate King is grinning delightedly.

"One day I'll take the Fire Stone for myself," he says. "And you're going to help me!"

The Pirate King seizes your arm and, to your horror, Tom, Elenna and the battle scene fade away. Sanpao's magic makes you reappear on the pirate ship. Dread washes over you as you realise that the vessel is soaring through the clouds.

Sanpao shoves a mop and bucket into your hands. "Oh yes," he sneers, "you'll help me destroy Avantia. But until then,

you're a slave on board my ship. Now, swab the deck!"

Your Quest has failed. Sanpao will destroy Avantia...

46

You lead the way across the marsh.
With each step you take, the mud makes
a slurping noise that reminds you of a
creature eating. You shudder.

The marsh is dotted with stagnant pools
with flies buzzing around them. Ahead,
a cloud of green mist hangs in the air.

"I don't like the look of that," says
Elenna, and Silver whines.

"Me neither," you agree. "But we've
got to keep going."

As you reach the mist, the air becomes
thicker. Soon you can only see a few paces
ahead. But through a gap in the green
cloud, you catch sight of movement.

"Someone's there," you whisper. Elenna
slides her bow from her shoulder and you
draw your sword. You prowl forwards,
moving as quietly as the squelching mud
allows.

A voice floats through the mist. "Who's
there – friend or foe?"

You and Elenna grin at each other as you recognise the speaker. "Tom!" you both shout.

Your friend emerges from the mist, leading Storm. "I thought you might be Sanpao's pirates," Tom says with a smile.

He shows you a cluster of bubbles rising from one of the stagnant pools. They disappear, then more bubbles appear in a pool nearby.

You gasp. "Something's breathing under the water!"

Tom nods. "It could be one of Sanpao's Beasts. Let's follow the trail of bubbles and find out."

"And stay near enough for it to attack?" cries Elenna. "No – let's find somewhere high up so we can see where the bubbles are leading."

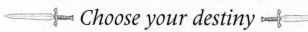 *Choose your destiny*

To follow the trail of bubbles, turn to **7**

To view the trail from somewhere high up, turn to **38**

47

You pick up the axe and Sanpao draws the cutlass from his belt.

"Let's finish this," you say through gritted teeth.

Sanpao swings his weapon at you in a flashing arc. You duck, feeling the rush of air as the blade passes over your head. With a flick of your wrist, you bring the axe upwards, slicing off the tip of the Pirate King's beard.

Sanpao growls. He jabs his cutlass at your chest, and you block his attack with the side of the axe-head. There's a clang of metal striking metal, and a crack appears on Sanpao's blade. *Now's my chance*, you realise.

The Pirate King swings his cutlass once more. As his blow falls, you raise the axe to meet it...

Craaaaaack! The cutlass shatters. Sanpao staggers back in shock, and then topples over. You stand over him, one booted foot on his chest, holding the axe to his throat.

Tom and Elenna cheer.

"Hand over the red gem you stole," you order, "and I'll spare your sorry skin."

The defeated Pirate King retrieves the Fire Stone from his pocket. You take it and let him sit up. "I've had enough of this realm," he grumbles.

"Be gone, then," says a voice. The air shimmers, and Aduro appears. He points his staff at Sanpao, and the Pirate King disappears in a puff of black smoke. The Good Wizard smiles at you. "Your Quest is over! Thanks to your bravery, Avantia is safe. Just one choice remains – to return the Fire Stone to the village yourself, or to let me take it back while you start the celebrations!"

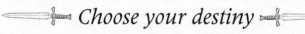 *Choose your destiny*

To return the Fire Stone to the village yourself, turn to **39**

To let Aduro return the Fire Stone while you start celebrating, turn to **50**

48

"Make for Shark Tooth Bay!" Sanpao
orders his crew. Smirking, he turns to you
and your friends. "The sharks there are so
vicious, they would attack a Beast."

The pirate ship flies over the Western
Ocean, following the line of the Avantian
coast. *We're not that far out to sea yet*, you
think. A plan springs into your head, and
you whisper it to Tom and Elenna.

"Come on, boy!" Elenna shouts to Silver.
They run down the plank and leap off the
end, and Tom follows on Storm.

"What's going on?" splutters Sanpao.
"Stop them!"

But it's too late. "We'll be back," you
warn Sanpao, then urge Lightning off the
plank too.

You fall through the air, down, down –
then plunge into the water, floating out of
Lightning's saddle. Kicking furiously, you
make for the surface. Tom and Elenna bob
nearby, and you can see the two horses,
their eyes wide. Silver paddles beside his
mistress.

"We did it!" you yell happily.

You strike out for shore. When your feet touch land, you take Lightning's reins and guide your brave horse onto the brightly coloured shingle.

Elenna gives a cry and points to a shark's fin moving through the water.

"We were just in time," Tom says.

But the fin comes closer. It rears up to reveal a Beast: a human skeleton with shark's teeth and fin, and webbed feet. Grey patches of skin and black rags hang from its ribcage.

"Do you dare fight Polkai the Shark-Man?" the Beast roars.

"We don't fear you, Polkai!" you reply. You wonder whether to fight the Beast in the water – or pretend one of the pebbles is the Fire Stone and lure Polkai onto land.

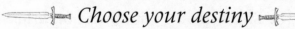 *Choose your destiny*

To fight the Beast in the water, turn to **5**

To lure the Beast onto land, turn to **14**

49

"Stay here," you whisper to Lightning. Leaving her at the foot of the cliff, you, Elenna and Silver climb up. The air echoes with the roars of the fighting Beasts.

Scrambling over a heap of rocks, you reach the top. The Beasts are directly beneath you. Arcta growls as the shark-Beast holds him in a headlock.

"You cannot defeat Polkai the Shark Man," snarls Sanpao's Beast. "I was destroyed once – but I will never lose again!"

"We'll see about that," you mutter. Grabbing a rock, you take aim at Polkai, and hurl it with all your might. It strikes the Beast's fin and he gives a bellow of pain. Arcta seizes his chance to break free from the Shark-Man's grip. Using his arms like clubs, he rains down punches on Polkai. The Shark-Man topples into the lake.

"This isn't over," Polkai yells, then

dives beneath the surface.

Arcta's hairy face crinkles in delight as he looks up to where you, Elenna and Silver stand on top of the cliff. He gives a roar, then heads off towards the mountains.

"I think that was a thank you," says Elenna with a grin. "I wonder what Polkai meant about already being destroyed once?"

"I'm not sure," you reply. "Let's go after him and find out."

But something brushes your shoulder. It's a coil of rope, dangling down from the clouds. Knotted to the end is a flag bearing the symbol of a skull.

Elenna's eyes are wide. "That's Sanpao's flag. Do you think we should climb up?"

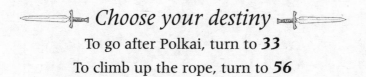

Choose your destiny

To go after Polkai, turn to **33**

To climb up the rope, turn to **56**

50

Aduro murmurs a spell. The Good Wizard and the scene of your battle fade. Everything turns blinding white, then you, Tom and Elenna reappear in the palace. In front of you sits King Hugo on his throne.

You bow and the King smiles. "It should be I who bow to you," he says. "News has reached me of your victory against Sanpao."

"I couldn't have done it without my friends," you say.

King Hugo claps his hands and servants bring in plates of meat and pastries. "Let the celebrations begin! After all," he adds, gesturing towards a window, "some have already started."

You look out into the courtyard, where Silver gnaws on a large bone, and Lightning and Storm munch on a trough full of oats.

We deserve to celebrate, you think. *But danger always threatens Avantia – and while there's blood in my veins, I'm ready to defeat it!*

The End

51

"No, you can't come with us," you tell the girl. Tom walks off down the path, leading his horse. You do the same with Lightning.

"Stop!" the girl yells. You look over your shoulder to see that she's holding the cutlass. "You were right," she says with a sneer. "This cutlass does belong to a pirate – me!"

She throws off the cloak to reveal a black tunic with Sanpao's skull symbol on the front. At her belt hangs a whip. You can see metal barbs glinting along its surface.

You and Tom draw your swords, but the pirate girl is faster. She flicks out her whip and it coils around you both, as tightly as a python. The barbs sink into your skin. You can't move.

The girl holds her cutlass to your neck. "Time to die, you scurvy fool..."

Your Quest has failed. Sanpao will destroy Avantia...

52

"No," you say. "I will not show mercy
to a Beast!"

Elenna puts a hand on your shoulder.
"Polkai was once human," she says.
"He might have some goodness
within him still. Isn't that worth
saving?"

You push her away. "Don't be
ridiculous!"

Swinging your sword like an axe, you
slice off Polkai's fin. He slumps to the
ground.

Tom shakes his head, too shocked to
speak. Elenna's fists are clenched. Even
Lightning turns away.

"I've done the right thing!" you shout.

But something grips your ankle like
a vice. It's Polkai.

"This isn't quite over," he hisses through
his cracked jaw. With his last scrap of
strength, he pulls you to the ground.
"There shall be no mercy for you either..."

The Beast's cutlass slashes. All becomes darkness.

Your Quest has failed. Sanpao will destroy Avantia...

53

"We don't want you on our Quest," you tell Polkai. "You're still a Beast."

The Shark-Man's eyes narrow. Anger sparks within them like hot coals. "Still a Beast," he repeats. "In that case, I had better behave like a Beast, hadn't I?"

He roars, showing his rows of jagged teeth, then seizes hold of your shoulders.

"Get off me!" You struggle, but his grip is too powerful.

"You shall suffer like I have," Polkai snarls. "You shall be as wretched as me!"

Elenna grabs Polkai's arm. "Please, don't hurt—"

But the Beast shrugs her off as easily as a fly. He tightens his grip on your shoulders and you feel blasts of magic shoot through his palms into you. You scream as your body twists and writhes. The skin between your fingers fuses to become webbed. New rows of teeth force their way through your gums. Your head throbs, and you feel the back of your skull crack as something forces its way through. *A fin*, you realise in horror. *A fin like his...*

Polkai grins. "Now you are a shark Beast too. And as I am your creator, you are cursed to follow my commands." He spins you towards Tom and Elenna. "And my first order, Beast, is that you kill your friends..."

Your Quest has failed. Sanpao will destroy Avantia...

54

Gripping the spear, you square up to Sanpao. The crystal tip glints in the sunlight. Tom and Elenna stand nearby, worry etched onto their faces.

"It's Sanpao you should be concerned about," you tell your friends. "He's

about to be defeated!"

"Silence!" snarls the Pirate King, seizing another spear. The veins in his tattooed arms stand out in ridges.

He's angry, you think. *If I can make him lose his temper, he won't fight properly...*

"Poor Sanpao," you say mockingly. "His Beast is gone, and soon he will be too. I pity him!"

"No one pities me!" Sanpao roars.

His eyes flash and he swings the spear wildly. You nimbly dart aside, and Sanpao's spear slams into the ground – shattering the crystal. The Pirate King is unarmed! You aim your own spear at his chest and Sanpao raises his hands in defeat.

"What do you want from me?" he asks.

"You must leave Avantia forever," you reply. "And hand over the red gem you stole from the mountain village."

Sanpao takes the Fire Stone from his pocket.

"Roll it towards Elenna," you order.

Sanpao does so, and Elenna puts it safely in her quiver.

"That trinket seems a small ransom," the Pirate King says. "I'll wager it's no ordinary gem."

You would love to tell Sanpao the truth about the Fire Stone – and that he let its powers slip through his fingers! But it might be wise to keep the secret to yourself...

⟝ *Choose your destiny* ⟞

To keep the Fire Stone's powers secret, turn to **39**

To tell Sanpao about the Fire Stone's powers, turn to **45**

55

Squelch! You slam the front of your shield down on a cluster of fire ants. Their bodies crunch, spraying you with red slime. Tom does the same with his shield, and even the horses stamp on them. But you can't destroy the ants quickly enough.

Further down the path glitters a stream of water. It gives you an idea...

"Over the stream!" you shout, and break into a run. Storm and Lightning leap easily over it, while you and Tom wade through. A few fire ants fall into the water and disappear with a fizzing sound. The other ants retreat.

"Phew," Tom says with a grin.

You're in a patch of dense undergrowth. Creepers cling to your clothes and wind around Tom's arms.

He frowns. "It's as if they're trying to trap us!"

Before you can answer, the ground trembles.

"What's happening?" you shout.

─────╼ *Choose your destiny* ╾─────

To escape from the creepers and flee, turn to **22**

To stay and find out why the ground is shaking,

turn to **3**

56

You grip the railing that runs around the deck of the pirate ship. One of the pirates is at the wheel, grinning as he makes the vessel lurch through the sky.

"Enjoying the ride, you fish-stinking fools?" he crows.

A wave of nausea surges up your throat, but you force it back down.

"I can't believe you're here too," Tom mutters to Elenna. "And Storm and Lightning."

The two horses stand miserably by a pile of barrels, transported magically onto the deck by Sanpao. More pirates surround you, their cutlasses raised. There are too many to fight.

We're their prisoners, you think. *Coming on board this ship was a huge mistake.*

The Pirate King himself sits sprawled in a throne made from animal bones. Beside him is a treasure chest overflowing with coins, goblets and jewels. You catch your

breath when you spot a red gem among
them – the Fire Stone!

Sanpao scoops up a handful of coins,
letting them trickle through his fingers.
"There's only one thing in this world as
great as me," he says. "And that's my
treasure."

"It's not yours," snaps Tom. "It belongs
to the people you've stolen it from –
innocent people of Avantia."

Sanpao's face turns as angry as a

thundercloud. He jumps up, his boots ringing across the deck as he strides towards Tom. "One more word out of you, you dung-brained, interfering toad," he growls, "and I'll throw you overboard. But that's only after I've made you beg for mercy. First, I'm going to snap your..."

As Sanpao goes on, the other pirates gather round to gawp.

They've forgotten about me, you think. *I've got to get the Fire Stone!*

You creep towards the treasure chest. Your heart races as you hope the pirates won't notice. When you're close enough, you reach out – but your fingers slip and send a pile of jewels clattering onto the deck!

Sanpao and the pirates spin round. "That's it!" Sanpao snarls. "You've tested my patience enough. You will all walk the plank!"

The crew whoop delightedly. "Please," you beg over the noise. "Spare my friends!"

"How noble," the Pirate King sneers.

"But I want to see you all fall to your deaths. Now, where would you like to fall – into the fire of the volcano, or into the ocean with the sharks?"

Choose your destiny

To walk the plank over the volcano, turn to **17**

To walk the plank over the ocean, turn to **48**

Fight the Beasts,
Fear the Magic

www.beastquest.co.uk

Have you checked out the Beast Quest website?
It's the place to go for games, downloads, activities,
sneak previews and lots of fun!

You can read all about your favourite beasts,
download free screensavers and desktop wallpapers
for your computer, and even challenge your friends
to a Beast Tournament.

Sign up to the newsletter at www.beastquest.co.uk
to receive exclusive extra content and the
opportunity to enter special members-only
competitions. We'll send you up-to-date info on all
the Beast Quest books, including the next exciting
series which features four brand-new Beasts!

All books priced at £4.99, special bumper editions priced at £5.99.

Orchard Books are available from all good bookshops, or can be ordered from our website: www.orchardbooks.co.uk, or telephone 01235 827702, or fax 01235 8227703.

FREE COLLECTOR CARDS INSIDE!

Series 9: THE WARLOCK'S STAFF
COLLECT THEM ALL!

Malvel is up to his evil tricks again! The fate of all the lands is in Tom's hands...

978 1 40831 316 9

MINOS
THE DEMON BULL

978 1 40831 317 6

KORAKA
THE WINGED ASSASSIN

978 1 40831 318 3

SILVER
THE WILD TERROR

978 1 40831 319 0

SPIKEFIN
THE WATER KING

978 1 40831 320 6

TORPIX
THE TWISTING SERPENT

978 1 40831 321 3

Series 10: MASTER OF THE BEASTS
COLLECT THEM ALL!

An old enemy has come back to haunt Tom –
and unleash six awesome new Beasts!

978 1 40831 518 7

978 1 40831 519 4

978 1 40831 520 0

978 1 40831 521 7

978 1 40831 522 4

978 1 40831 523 1

FREE
COLLECTOR
CARDS
INSIDE!

Series 11: THE NEW AGE
COMING SOON!

Avantia and all the known worlds are under
threat by a deadly enemy! Can Tom survive?

978 1 40831 841 6

978 1 40831 842 3

978 1 40831 843 0

978 1 40831 844 7

978 1 40831 845 4

978 1 40831 846 1

BEAST QUEST SPECIALS
COLLECT THEM ALL!

Join Tom and his brave companions for these
Beast Quest special bumper editions, with two
stories in one

978 1 84616 951 9

978 1 84616 994 6

978 1 40830 382 5

978 1 40830 436 5

978 1 40830 735 9

978 1 40830 736 6

978 1 40831 027 4

978 1 40831 517 0

Join Tom on his Beast Quests
and take part in a terrifying adventure
where YOU call the shots!